FSC
www.fsc.org
MIX
Papier aus ver-
antwortungsvollen
Quellen
Paper from
responsible sources
FSC® C105338

English proofreader:
Susan Harris-Mittelstädt
on behalf of JP Translations,
Übersetzungsbüro Jana Paul,
Oberhausen, www.jptranslations.com

Illustration & Layout:
Walburga Weigmann

Manufactured and published by:
Books on Demand GmbH, Norderstedt, Germany
ISBN 978-3-8423-7853-7

Acknowledgements

I would like to thank my friend Walburga Weigmann who during the completion of this little book assisted me with literary advice and her caring eye for detail, looked after the artistic layout and selected the oil paintings used for its illustration. I also want to thank my translator co-worker Susan Harris-Mittelstädt for taking care of the English-speaking editorial with a lot of personal verve, supporting me very much in the use of idiomatic phrases and her empathy during the entire creative process. Without your help this very personal book project would have been impossible.

Jana Paul

For my son Joshua

Table of Contents

The Calumet 8

The Cloud Painter 18

The little Butterfly and the Cornflower 26

The little Hand 30

The Sandman and the Sweets Party 44

The Moon Pony 60

The Star that wanted to be Famous 70

Chief in a Cave, oil on canvas

The Calumet

nce upon a time, when the Earth was young and the moon still a little kid dancing around her, the chiefs of all the native Indian tribes gathered to enjoy the soothing smoke of their first pipe, a calumet carved by a mighty pipe maker called Eagle Spirit. The chiefs were in awe of the fragile pipe that displayed the symbol of Eagle Spirit's tribe as well as those of befriended clans and tribes, as this pipe was the first to be lit and passed on in their gatherings, to inhale the smoke of peace and friendship together and listen intently to each other's tales until the sky went dark and the stars had gone to sleep.

Many years passed and Eagle Spirit's calumet listened to many stories told by the old chiefs and the pipe maker. The favourite pipe was passed from mouth to mouth and grew accustomed to their different smells and tastes and ways of talking and thinking. The calumet never judged, but listened, and when its smoke went straight up into the air it was listening very intently, and when the smoke was blurred it was getting quite confused by the words the chiefs were uttering into the night. Sometimes, it heard weird and wonderful stories about animals and spirits while at other times it heard jokes about other people, not in a jeering way but light-heartedly laughing with each other and having fun. The calumet freely gave its tobacco smoke which the native Indians inhaled deeply while making satisfied noises, and it was rewarded with a story of beauty and wisdom every time it gave its inspiring smoke to them. In turn, the calumet was filled with their spirit and learnt about the ways of the world, nature and animals, young kids and the elders, and about life and death. The calumet never grew tired of listening, nor did the chiefs grow tired of talking and slowly but surely, the calumet turned into more than just a tool, it became a friend among friends.

One night, the oldest chief seemed to be very alarmed and his usual poised nature and good temper were out of balance. He did not carefully select the tobacco and herbs for their usual ceremony of storytelling this time but hastily stuffed the powder into the pipe and drew a deep breath himself, then another, and forgot to pass it on to his neighbour. The other chiefs saw this and were confused, eager to get to know the trouble the older chief was about to tell them. He thoughtfully turned the calumet in his hands, watching the symbols of the clans dancing with each other. Then he looked up and grimly told the other chiefs: "A war lies ahead... The smoke has darkened and the clouds bear a heavy burden, it will rain and rain and the tears of our people will mingle with it. Tonight, I have to tell you a story that is not pleasing, one that will make history, and we have to accept that tonight will be the last night we meet." The other chiefs were aghast, taken by surprise, and talked confusedly, not understanding what was going on. Slowly, the old chief took the talking stick and began to speak. The others fell silent, keen to listen. The old chief put the calumet in the centre of their meeting place as he was talking, lit a fire, and started to burn the calumet. "Why are you doing that"? the youngest of the chiefs cried, alarmed. He was scared, watching the calumet burn, its final smoke turning white and silvery, the thickening threads flowing into the open night sky. "I am burning our stories before history burns us out", the chief replied gravely, "and we will put the ashes in our vessels and carry them home to our wives and children, who will take care of the ashes until the Earth is again ready to listen to another calumet, made by another honest and brave pipe maker. When the time is right, the calumet will rise from its ashes and speak again to remind us about the ancient stories and traditions, but now we need to protect ourselves and leave no trace of what is dear to us. The Trail of Tears will be hard for most of us but when we walk along it, searching for our new home, the women will chant and carry these ashes with them. And every old, ill or weak person will not have to worry as the stronger and fitter of us will leave a trail of ashes for them to show the way in case they are left behind. – Now go and prepare yourselves, the white man will come and we need to be ready for our long walk." The chief rose with dignity and the other men also stood up in awe. The calumet was gone and a small pile of silvery ashes remained, a heap of stories, ready to be carried on to fill new homes with hope and reminiscence. The chief filled each small vessel with a small portion of the ashes and they parted, each one leaving in the Wind direction they had come from, carrying one of the vessels.

When they reached their homes, the soldiers had already arrived and grief and sadness fell upon the native Indian tribes who had to leave their homelands against their will. They did not know what was facing them, nor did they fully understand what they would have to leave behind. It was like a bad dream and for days on end they had to walk long distances, the paths they travelled on marked with their blood and tears. Again and again, older people and women with young children were forced to stay behind and the chiefs poured some of the collected ashes along the track in order to show them the way and help them to stay in contact. They did this in the hope that they would not lose them, to create a visible bond they could follow to stay in touch. But suddenly the Wind changed … and it blew the ashes in every direction so the people who had been left behind could no longer see where the ash trail was clearly, making them lose their way.

The Wind was sad about what it had done, and promised to be their friend from now on and never again betray the native Indian people. It started to gently blow warm air around them, to guide them towards hope and make the children feel at home again, despite all the trouble and hardship they had suffered. It created wind behind them to carry them forward, and it caressed their arms to make them strong again. And the Indians never lost hope, and they forgave the Wind. After all, the Wind had always been their mother and knew everything.

Many years after they had settled into their new homeland in Oklahoma, a young pipe maker came along and the chiefs of the tribes again gathered in remembrance of the elders and the old traditional ways. A new, ornate calumet was ceremoniously carved and filled with sacred smoke, then the youngest of them inhaled a deep breath of it. "I am innocent," he said, "but I want to learn about the stories of our elders. I want to know who I am and where I came from." Then he passed the pipe on to the eldest of them. The elders smiled, and the oldest chief took the calumet. "Is there anything more to say ...?" he asked the group gathered around him. Hesitantly, a younger chief from the Wind Clan produced a small vessel from his one of his pockets and, with a gentle touch of an eagle's feather, he honoured the dead people who had lost their lives walking the Trail of Tears. Then he opened the vessel. The Wind blew gently and the ashes were scattered in all directions again, this time on purpose. The chief stood up, raising his arms into the sky, and with a loud and strong voice he said: "Our ashes have been spread far and wide in this Universe, as have our stories, and forever shall they be passed on from father to son, and mother to daughter, and sister to brother. So be it, and a new dawn has arrived for our people, just as our breath will never stop being used to tell our stories or to carry their ashes, never to be forgotten, but transformed into new stories every time we smoke the calumet, and every day we will dance and sing, and walk the earth in joy and gratitude. The Great Spirit has shown us the way again and no-one who believes will be left behind."

They sat in a circle, pressing new, sacred tobacco into the new calumet, passing it from one to the other. And after many sad old stories, some happier ones followed and, after hours, someone told such a funny and wonderful story that they all broke into giggles and then outright laughter. The stars blinked and that night a strong and resilient nation showed that nothing on earth could take away their laughter and that nothing on earth could oust them from their inner home.

Spanish Moss (detail), oil on canvas

18

The Cloud Painter

Once upon a time there was a little boy brimming with imagination who loved to go out into the meadows straight after a big storm to watch the clouds moving and the tree tops swinging. He would lie down under his favourite gnarled tree, which he called the Chieftain Tree because he knew it had once been a beacon tree for the Indians to guide them to the portage routes in the same way as a lighthouse would guide big ships into the harbour. This big Chieftain Tree was the boy's secret refuge as well as a close friend under which he could silently watch the different hues and shapes of the clouds that were being driven by the wind across the sky like little white and black sheep being chased by a watchful but wild and strong sheepdog. Whenever possible, the young lad talked to his tree and asked him questions, and only he could understand what his old friend told him because he had the ability to listen carefully and observe attentively, and his eyes and little heart were wide open to Nature to let in the whispers of the boughs and leaves, and the touch of the breezes that were as precious to him as his dearest friends and family.

One day, after the final roll of thunder had announced that the worst of the tempest had retreated, the boy went out to play his favourite game again, laying down under the big gnarled old tree to watch the clouds gathering and then scattering anew like excited ants, not knowing where to go until the gentle breezes and the faraway barking of that sheepdog of the skies brought them back into line again, ready for their journey and heavenly dances. The boy watched them for a while, the hues and shades ranging from the deepest leaden grey to a silvery lining around the most beautiful of the clouds, as well as warm and funny rosy ones, and threatening and towering blackish ones that frightened him a little bit, although he felt safe with his big Chieftain Tree friend to guard him and gave him shelter. There were also fluffy white ones that really looked like the little sheep he used to count when he could not fall asleep, and there were those weird ones with no shape at all that looked like torn pieces of gauze or the cotton balls that covered his floor and bed following a pillow fight with his brother after their nightly prayers. The snowflakes were there, too, those clouds that used to chatter and chuckle with him and were unruly and disobeyed the sheepdog, which had to bark louder and push harder to make them join the flock. Even so, the poor dog never managed to get them all together as one or the other of them would always giggle and start to dance out of line again.

Sometimes the young lad would close his eyes for a short time so he could reopen them in wonder and shriek with pleasure when he saw that the clouds wanted to play his favourite game with him. The wind had been tamed too and joined in their game by blowing the clouds into different shapes. The boy watched them transform into animals he recognised most of the time, although at other times he could not make out their earlier or new shapes at all, but he always viewed the spectacle with awe and joy because he could lose himself in dreams and the beautiful, changing play of colours, shapes and movements.

This day was different though, the leaves were talking and singing another tune and the Chieftain Tree was nodding its head in wonder and wisdom. The youngster was day-dreaming, he was tired too, and thinking about the story his Mum had told him the day before. A little smile touched his lips as he remembered her soft arms around him and almost heard her gentle voice as she talked to him, and he felt utterly content, loved and cosy. He imagined his mother was next to him, watching the sky with him, and he exclaimed: "Mum, can you see the little tiger cloud high up there?" – He could see his mother smiling again, nodding her head in unison with the Chieftain Tree and he thought for a moment that the waving boughs of his tree friend were his mother's arms embracing him. Then he heard his Mum reply: "Yes, but look, the little tiger is crying – it wants you to paint it into a real jungle tiger with bright orange and black stripes, you should get a ladder and start painting it." The boy laughed happily and started painting the tiger cloud and he could feel the cloud's teardrops dry as his brush touched it, and the sun came out from behind a cloud to chuckle while the tiger cloud was being given its new colours. But then the wind suddenly changed and - oooops – the tiger cloud changed into a rabbit and the rabbit started to cry about this funny pelt of orange and black stripes, and the boy scratched his head and started painting again. He used the loveliest white he could find among the cloud-coloured paints in his bucket and soon the little rabbit was happy as its hide had changed into a wonderful glowing white furry mass and it joyfully hopped away with the wind. Then the boy saw a dolphin swimming by and he quickly changed to the greyish blue colour and gave it a shiny finish, and the dolphin thanked him and swam on to proudly show its electric blue fin off to all its cloudy mates. The wind dried them off with a cool movement of its hands. The boy stood on his ladder all day long until the sky was a sea of colours and hues and everyone could see how beautiful the creatures were that the boy had coloured with his paintbrush.

Then dusk slowly crept in and the boy's eyes started to hurt a bit and he suddenly felt terribly tired. It grew darker and darker and the boy was afraid he might not find his way home. The bright clouds were being transformed into the greyish shadows of the creatures of the night that were scurrying about to gather food or look for a suitable hiding place for a good nights' sleep. The boy had a thoughtful look on his face for a moment but then he smiled and, while he was saying goodbye to his old gnarled friend, he climbed onto the cloud ladder one last time to paint a huge silver disc, as it was a dark night without a moon. The Chieftain Tree laughed out loud and shook his head in disbelief, making the leaves tickle each other and make funny rustling noises. The boy grinned back at the Chieftain Tree until he heard his Mum calling him, then he climbed down his ladder quickly and stowed it away before making his way home for supper with his little hands stuffed in his pockets.

All around the world, children in their beds could watch that bright silver moon smiling down at them, and none of them was afraid of ghosts that night because, as all children know, the moon is their protector and, if they are lucky enough to see a full moon, they know that the Chieftain Tree will be waiting outside for them to climb up that ladder and paint golden stars, too, one for each child, which all need to be polished so that they are happy, lucky stars.

Blue Flower, oil on canvas

The little Butterfly and the Cornflower

Once upon a time there was a beautiful little butterfly that enjoyed flying to and fro among the flowers in the bright sunshine the whole day. His favourite one was a tiny, delicate little cornflower. One day, the butterfly told his friend that he wanted to fly high up into the sky to visit one of the white clouds up there. This made the cornflower feel terribly sad, because she could not join the butterfly in this adventure and she was afraid that he would never come back. But the butterfly's wish to visit the white cloud in the sky was so strong that he ignored her fears and said goodbye to the cornflower before starting on his journey. He had not gone far before he discovered that his tender wings were too weak and they could not carry him very far. A passing strong wind with a kind heart saw his difficulty and made a promise. "I will take you to the cloud, little butterfly, come with me, you can trust me". And when the butterfly spread his wings again, the strong wind blew harder and harder until the little butterfly reached his friend, the big white cloud, who was delighted to have the little butterfly's company. They smiled happily at each other and enjoyed their time together until nightfall. The little butterfly then needed to be taken back to earth but the wind had stopped blowing because he had gone to sleep. The butterfly cried bitterly because he could not go back to see his tiny friend, the gentle cornflower, and suddenly big tears rolled down from the white cloud that had become darker, sharing the butterfly's sorrow. Down on earth, in the meadow, the cornflower waited and waited and became sadder and sadder. When the teardrops fell on her petals, she knew that her best friend was trapped and that the butterfly was crying. The tiny cornflower summoned the strong wind and asked it for help, and the strong wind obligingly blew once more so the butterfly could be carried back to the meadow. Safely back home, the little butterfly saw the teardrops on the petals that the cornflower had lovingly preserved like precious diamonds. The butterfly kissed the cornflower, and they remained friends forever. The white cloud, slumbering now, smiled upon them in its dream, and the little butterfly soared and danced among the flowers and kissed his favourite friend while the wind blew around them warmly and gently.

Lake Erie (detail), oil on canvas

The Little Hand

One evening, a little boy was walking through a thick forest with his Mum. She held onto him and told him to stay right by her side because the forest was dark and wild and they had to walk for a while before they reached their home. So she took the boy's little hand in her big, warm one to lead him safely through the forest.

When night fell, his Mum was walking so far to get home quickly that the boy suddenly lost her big hand in the darkness and fell over a root that was sticking out of the forest path. He lost his balance and rolled over the edge of the tiny path and down the hillside. He was so covered with muddy and wet leaves from the gully he had fallen into that his voice was muffled when he screamed so his Mum could not hear him properly in the dark night. From afar, he could hear her scared voice but it faded after some time as she desperately searched for her little son, moving further away from him without realising it.

After the shock had subsided, the little boy stood up, shook the leaves off his tiny body and tried to gain a foothold in the wet, muddy ground. Slowly, he laboured uphill again, stumbling over roots and mouse holes, unable to see his own little hands before him in the darkness of the thick forest. He was shouting and trying to find his Mum but she was even further away by now, still looking for him and out of sight. After hopelessly searching and shouting for some time, the little boy was so exhausted and scared he started to cry. He felt terribly lonely it was so dark and he missed his mother's big, warm hand that had protected him all the time. Now he was alone, lost in the deep, dark forest, trying to make his way home somehow. But there was no signpost to show him the way and no-one to ask, so he sat down below a huge gnarled oak tree and tried to find some comfort and shelter.

Suddenly, some branches broke above him and something like nuts rattled down on his head. "Ouch." the boy exclaimed, looking up. A little squirrel was leaping around in the tree, moving up and down it excitedly. "Hello, little squirrel", the boy said politely, "can you show me the way home? I've lost my mother's big, warm hand, I feel really lonely and need some help to find my way back." But the squirrel turned away angrily and replied: "Can't you see I am busy collecting nuts and acorns for the winter, I cannot help you, you cheeky boy." Then it disappeared into the trees, in a hurry and flurry. The poor boy thought: "What an unfriendly little squirrel... I'm so lonely and I need a guide to show me the way home but the squirrel didn't like me or want to help so I need to keep moving and find another guide somewhere." The silver moon came out from behind the dark night clouds as if it was concerned, too and its mild, cold light showed the boy where to walk and climb and how to avoid falling over roots and hurting himself on thorns and branches hanging low from the trees in a threatening way. The boy looked up into the sky and thanked the milky, silver moon for shedding its light and he thought gratefully that he had at least found one friend at last. After a while, he passed a fox den and the cheeky little nose of a curious fox cub appeared. It was turning its head from side to side and the light from the moon transformed the little fox cub into a ghostly shadow. The little boy shrieked when the face of the father fox appeared next to the dancing nose of its fox cub. Then he pulled himself together and asked politely: "Father fox, you are very clever and certainly know the forest, can you show me the way home, please. I lost my mother's big, warm hand in the dark, I'm lonely and hungry, I need to find my way back very soon. My Mum will be very worried now." Father fox looked up and mumbled: "My dear boy, I have a little fox cub to look after tonight, I'm sorry but I can't come with you to show you the way. You look like a big, brave boy to me and I'm sure you'll find your way home quickly by yourself." Then it pushed its fox cub back into the fox den and disappeared. The boy started to cry again. "No-one is willing to help me, I feel so lonely, there surely must be a guide somewhere that is friendly and nice that could show me the way out of this dark, thick forest. I need to keep moving and find a friend, and some help." The moon gave him a sad smile from above, and the unhappy little boy stumbled on in tears. "At least the moon is helping me", he thought, just as something became visible between the bushes and trees in the shadowy twilight. "Oh Mr. Barn Owl", the boy shouted gratefully, "You surely know the way out of the forest, you are a wise bird and very friendly, I've read about you in my picture books. I'm so glad to meet you here and would like to ask you if you can give me some advice." But Mr. Barn Owl blinked with half-open eyes and sadly shook its head. "I'm sorry, dear", it replied in a low, mumbling voice. "I'm old and tired and I've lost my glasses. They were my only pair of glasses, and now I can hardly see the way myself. I'm truly sorry, but I can't help you. You look like a big, clever boy to me and you'll soon will find your way back home."

The boy was beginning to feel really desperate. "Not even the wise owl can help me," he thought to himself sadly, "is there no- guide to help me in dark, thick forest?" The moon's pale disc glowed upon him and the boy felt its love and concern. He thought of his mother and tried hard not to lose hope. Mr. Barn Owl settled its wings back into place and closed its eyes to go back into its dozy half-sleep without its glasses. Suddenly the boy felt sorry for the wise old owl that seemed to be even more helpless than himself. "I'll come back soon and bring you a new pair of glasses," he promised, waving good-bye to the shadowy bird that was perched on a low bough in the twilight. He felt a bit better now and could detect some strength coming back into him.

Then, suddenly, a lone, grey wolf was standing on a nearby hillock in the night, howling wistfully at the silver moon. It turned its head slowly when the little boy appeared, giving a short, threatening growl. But the boy was courageous and he spoke in a firm, ringing voice. "Dear wolf, I know you are a wild and dangerous creature of the forest, although you are surely very clever and smart. I hope you can show me the way home because I've lost my way and my mother is crying and waiting for me to come back." The grey wolf was flattered, but growled threateningly again. "Hmmmmmm…. What will you give me in return for this favour? " he barked craftily. The boy's heart sank. "I have nothing to give you, dear wolf, I'm only a little boy, I'm lost and lonely, I'm sorry.. I have nothing of any value that I could give you in return for your favour." The wolf angrily jumped up and shook its big grey head, giving another loud, disgruntled howl. "Well I'm sorry, boy", he sneered, "I can't help you then. I know the way of course, but I want something in return. I'm a bad wolf, and I won't help you." The boy started to cry bitterly again. He could not understand why the wolf didn't want to help him but he had nothing to give the wolf so he needed to carry on. At least the wolf hadn't eaten him or attacked him, so the boy said goodbye and walked away. In the darkness he heard the fading howl of the wolf, and, looking up at the sky through a gap in the trees, he could see that the pale milky face of the silver moon looked sorrowful, too.

Finally, the disheartened boy was so tired that he fell over a molehill hidden by leaves. A grubby little jet-black mole was busy digging its way up out of the hill with its clawed forepaws and its velvety nose appeared, quivering in the cool air. A bitter tear fell from the boy's cheek at that very moment and landed on the mole's nose. It looked up at the little boy with interested, shiny eyes. "Why are you crying?" it asked kindly in a squeaky voice, its curiousity winning over its natural shyness. "Oh little mole, I'm so afraid and lonely, I've lost my way and my mother's big, warm hand in the dark forest." the miserable boy sobbed. "I've met so many unfriendly animals in the forest and none of them could help me or wanted to give me advice." The little mole bent its head thoughtfully and then whispered in an unsure little voice:" I think I can help you... I dig all the time and my underground runs lead the way to the other side of the forest. I know where people live, and I know where you have to go to find your Mum." The boy's heart jumped for joy and he suddenly felt extremely happy and hopeful for the first time. But then he asked fearfully: "But little mole, I'm only a small boy and I've got nothing to give you in return for your favour. Will you still show me the way out of the dark, thick forest? " The little mole smiled. "Don't worry", it said, coming closer. "I'm sure you can give me something." The young boy sadly shook his head. "I have nothing that would be of use to you, little mole, what could I could give you, what do you want?" The tiny mole moved even closer to sit by the little boy and replied: "Little boy... I'm a lonely mole and most of the time I live in my underground tunnels. I don't have many friends in the forest and I have to hide a lot. I feel lonely too. I would like a gentle little hand like yours to stroke me for a while so that I feel that I have a friend. I would like to feel your little, warm hand on my moleskin and I am grateful that you stumbled over my molehill." The little boy was taken by surprise and felt a lot of compassion for the little, lonely jet-black mole, being so familiar with loneliness himself now. Carefully and slowly, he reached down towards the little animal and touched its back. The little mole smiled contentedly. The youngster sat down and put the mole on his lap, humming a soft tune. His tiny little hand stroked the mole's little body and touched its nose gently with his finger. The mole laughed happily. "Now," it said, "I'll show you the way out of the forest. You are a very charming boy and I know I've now found a friend in the dark forest." The boy was happy now, too. He bent his head and listened to the advice the little mole gave him. "Just follow the molehills with the moon in front of you", the little mole said, "they will guide you right into the garden of your Mum's house. I'm sure she'll be sitting at the kitchen window waiting for you to come home." The little boy jumped up, feeling very grateful and happy. "Thank you so much, little mole", he said, beaming at it. "You're welcome," the mole grinned back. "Maybe I'll visit you in your garden now and then and you can stroke me with your warm little hands again, it felt so good, and then we can be friends and I'll tell you all about the latest news from the forest." The boy laughed again before quickly saying goodbye. The silver moon was half covered by dark night clouds again but there was still just enough light to make out the tiny molehills that were scattered on the ground, partly covered with leaves. The boy slowly followed them, making sure to keep the moon in front of him, and indeed, they led him out of the forest and into his own familiar garden. From afar, he could see that a light was on in the kitchen and when he got home the door flew open and his mother came running out with outstretched arms. "Thank Goodness you're back," she cried, and the boy cried too, he was so relieved, but when the tears subsided he smiled and told his Mum about the little mole and that it should be allowed to stay in the garden and be his friend. His mother laughed and agreed readily. And till this day the black velvety mole comes into the garden every now and then to visit its friend and tell him about the latest news from the forest. And then the little boy eats ice cream in the garden with the contented mole on his lap, his warm little hand gently stroking the mole's soft skin.

House by the Lake, oil on canvas

Blossom Dream, oil on canvas

The Little Sandman and the Sweets Party

nce upon a time, there was a little sandman kid who had just turned 5, the right age for a young sandman to join his father, the old sandman, to help him carry the huge sandbag filled with sleeping sand from the Moon to make kids sleep tight at night and to bless them with beautiful dreams.

The sandman kid was mischievous but curious, too. He felt very excited when the old sandman told him to fetch the finely-spun bag and bring it to the magic sand-pit that was filled with golden sparks from the dreamsand. The old sandman was a bit worried because someone would have to go to the Moon again soon to get some more dreamsand as the sand-pit was nearly empty. But the quantity of sand was still enough for one more visit down to Earth and the old sandman knew that it was very important to be punctual because otherwise the kids wouldn't want to go to bed and this would make their parents angry. So he showed his son how to fill the fine bag to the brim with dreamsand and how a tiny hole in the bag would make the sand dribble out of the bag slowly so that any wild animals that might follow the sandman on his way would fall asleep when attempting to pull at the sandman's dotted trousers to stop him or catch his attention. This often happened at homes where people kept their dogs outside in a kennel because they were usually still awake when the sandman arrived to make the kids fall asleep. The dogs were usually very curious as well as wild and distrustful sometimes too, and so the old sandman had developed a strategy to get rid of them for his own safety by letting some dreamsand trickle out of the sandbag. It was sort of funny because wherever he went he left a trail of sleeping dogs as well as cats along the way to the children's rooms. Usually the old sandman took the quickest route over the rooftops and through windows but at times it was quite a tough job to get the locked doors open ifthe kids had been mischievous and their parents had locked their doors as punishment. Then it got quite tricky because the old sandman had to make the parents fall asleep first so he could then secretly pinch the key to the children's rooms. This was not at all easy and he often needed loads of dreamsand to make the older people close their eyes. Sometimes the sandbag became empty far too fast and the poor old sandman would have to go back to his special planet where the magic sandpit was to get more dreamsand for the night. At times, he fell asleep himself during this procedure, it was so tiresome, but then as a result even more doors were locked the following evening because usually the kids who hadn't had any sleep were really mischievous and wouldn't stop nagging and teasing their parents. This led to even more doors being locked as punishment in the following days and the old sandman often thought that it was all a vicious circle but there was no other choice. One night, though, he had had enough of this game and asked his little son to help him make the kids fall asleep to get everyone out of trouble. The little sandman kid was exhilarated and very enthusiastic and he eagerly helped to carry the huge sandbag that was resting on his Dad's shoulders before it was thumped down into the shiny Dreamcar that helped them to transport the sandbag down to Earth. Some golden sparks flew around when the old sandman started the car and, once it was moving forward slowly, the dreamsand began to trickle slowly from the tiny hole to leave its dreamy sprinkling for the dangerous animals that might follow their path. At times a young and therefore curious little star would try to follow them, too but the dreamsand was very dangerous for them because it often made them fall fast asleep on the spot and then the little stars fell down to Earth like stones. The children on Earth were then told to make a wish because they had seen a shooting star or thought they had seen a comet falling down to Earth at high speed. This was wonderful fun for the kids, the sandman thought, but it was usually very tough for the poor little stars that fell on their butts and were then woken from their beautiful slumber all of a sudden by the hard bump. "It's not my problem." the old sandman thought, sighing, "They simply shouldn't be so curious." While kissing his little son on his dreamy cheeks, he changed into highspeed gear and off they went, disappearing into space in a cloud of golden sparks.

The little sandman was so mischievous sometimes that his old Dad had to use some of his golden dreamsand to make his own son fall asleep, but on this particular day he decided it would be better to make him work hard to make him want to fall asleep naturally. The old sandman grinned to himself as he imagined his little son sleeping all day long the following day, exhausted from helping him make the sand flow into the children's eyes, and watch out for cats and dogs, and hop into cupboards to look for hidden keys, and push against half-closed windows and even to find homeless kids who had wandered through secluded woodland and meadows trying to find a place to rest or a park bench to sleep on.s No, it was not an easy job to be a sandman sometimes, the old father thought, sighing. But he loved his job, just as he loved the children with their rosy cheeks, the way they were so cute and sweet lying in their beds, breathing softly. "It is a perfect job", he smiled to himself, "and yes, I am a born sandman. Let's hope my son will also be a great sandman one day, a sandman to be remembered and a sandman able to find the best golden moonsand for beautiful dreams", because there was also that slightly greyish moonsand that often brought worries and tears at night. Sandmen had to go through a long period of training in order to be able to tell the difference between them and only to fetch the right sand for the children. Now the little sandman's time had come to go through just the same apprenticeship and to learn from his father how to become a good sandman who would be loved by all children and parents alike one day.

Their journey came to an end as the first rooftops appeared and the lake and the first farmhouses came into sight. It was mid summer and the evening sun had also just been given some dreamsand to make it rub its tired eyes and emit the last warm and dark orange rays, tickling the moon that chuckled from afar, starting to radiate a lustrous milky glow that transformed the green and blossoming landscape into a magical sleepy world of soft hues of pale rose, yellowcool blue. "How beautiful," the little sandman kid exclaimed happily, his smile so wide it revealed a gap in his front teeth where one of his baby teeth had fallen out. He had hidden the precious tooth in his magic toothbox so the tooth fairy would come and make his wish come true and it finally had come true, the little sandman giggled, as his wish had been to be big and strong enough to accompany his father on his evening visits to the children's houses and this morning, when he had checked his toothbox, the little milk tooth had disappeared and his Dad had told him at breakfast that he would be going with him that very evening. The little sandman kid had laughed and sung aloud and was simply in a really good mood the whole day and even more so when his Dad told him to help him to carry the sandbag and step into the Dreamcar with him.

Now the old sandman whispered "Ssshhh!", holding his finger to his lips, and the little sandman lowered his head in awe and expectation. They hid their car behind a big fir tree nearby so that nobody would find it and then the old sandman shouldered his sandbag full of dreamsand. He told the young sandman kid to keep a finger pressed against the hole so that the dreamsand couldn't dribble out and leave a suspicious trail until they were far enough away from the secret place where they had parked their Dreamcar. The little sandman followed his Dad's instructions, and they set off towards the first house, which was easy to get into, luckily. There were no dogs, no cats, no mice, no curious little birds that would start chirping and make a big fuss.

"Look!" the little sandman cried, pointing through a window towards the garden of the house, which was decorated with brightly coloured balloons and ribbons and many sleeping bags that had been spread out around the lawn. Obviously the kids had just celebrated a birthday and were now getting ready for bed, which meant that they were being allowed to stay outside in the garden and tell each other stories and enjoy the adventure of spending the warm summer night in the garden. However, this would mean hard work for the old sandman and his son as it was obvious that nobody would want to go to sleep and miss out on all the fun.

"Oh no!", the old sandman groaned, but he was of course prepared for such an occasion. They hid in the flowerbeds where the fragrant, dark red sweet peas were already bowing their heads at the smell of the golden dreamsand and the peonies and roses also closed their petals and went to sleep at the sight of the two sandmen crouching near them. A little butterfly sneezed when the sand powdered it and lowered its wings to find rest under a huge sunflower. The little sandman beamed. "This is easy!" he declared, and his Dad laughed. "Wait, the kids are coming out now and you'll see that you'll have a much harder job with them." Then he suddenly went pale. "Oh my!", the old sandman exclaimed. "You haven't kept your finger pressed to the hole in the sandbag and now all the sand has gone and there will be a wild party here soon with no sand to make the children fall asleep!" "Yippy", the little sandman whooped happily, and produced a bag of sweets and candy because he had also prepared himself for all emergencies. "Maybe the sugar will calm them down and make then sleepy, Dad, and anyway, it is a birthday party tonight. We should share in the fun with them, don't you think?" The old sandman groaned again. Then the terrace door flew open and about ten kids in pyjamas came tumbling out, giggling and whispering to each other, looking for his or her sleeping bag to snuggle into. Shortly after, the tired but happy mother appeared and, sitting cross-legged in the middle of them,, started to quietly read a good night story to them which was about Mr. Sandman who would come and sprinkle sand over them to make them fall fast asleep. All of the kids giggled and wriggled about, not in the least bit tired, and the young sandman and old sandman groaned quietly in the flowerbeds. This was obviously the sign to start throwing the dreamsand into the children's eyes yet the sandbag was empty now and there was no way to make the kids close them. "Maybe time will help", the old sandman thought to himself, sighing. To make matters even worse, the little sandman had put his small bag full of sweets down somewhere between the roses and their thorns were trying to grab the candy because roses love sweets and sugar, too. The mother, noticing that the children were so restless, got up and went back into the house to get some soothing music just as one of the kids suddenly spotted the bag almost hidden in the rosebed next to him and wriggled out of his sleeping bag to grab it . "What a lovely surprise", the little boy shrieked happily and hurried back to the other kids to show them the contents of the bag. "This is wonderful", a girl with blonde braids and ribbons chuckled, grabbing a piece of candy rock, while her neighbour tried to catch a piece of chocolate. "Ssshhhhhh!", an older boy whispered, "We'll have to be quiet because I'm sure we're not supposed to be eating sweets so late in the evening now... Remember, we've brushed our teeth already..." The children fell silent, although some still couldn't suppress a quiet chuckle. The sweets were handed round and the kids happily munched them. Some started to invent stories about the sandman while the old and young sandmen were still desperately crouching low to remain hidden in the flowerbeds. "Now see what you've done, my son, the tooth fairies will be angry with us now as well as the parents. We need to rush back and fetch some more moonsand, let's hurry!" the old sandman scolded in an angry voice. The little sandman kid nodded slowly and thoughtfully. He hadn't given a thought to the tooth fairies when he had put the candy bag in his pocket. But now he thought about it, it was true, it was always a problem if kids' teeth fell out when they were not meant to and then the fairies couldn't fulfil the children's wishes either. On the contrary, most of the time the kids went through a hard time at the dentist's afterwards and that was not what the little sandman had intended at all. He had only wanted to make the kids happy but now it was time to put an end to the sweets party.

While the old sandman was still considering which road would be the quickest to the moon to get some more moonsand, some noise could be heard in sunflower border all of a sudden. Ten little dwarfs were approaching, apparently coming back from their work in the gemmines. The little sandman gaped, he had never seen a dwarf before. The dwarfs were carrying little lamps that were lit by glowworms and it was like a dancing performance of sparkling shadows. "What are they up to?" the little sandman whispered. His Dad shook his head in wonder. "I guess they're going to rescue us, they'll help us to make the kids fall asleep". The little sandman stared in surprise butthen saw that each dwarf was carrying a little toothbrush and the biggest dwarf was carrying strawberry-flavoured toothpaste.

The children were all in their sleeping bags again and had stopped munching sweets. They were half asleep because the bees had tried to help, too, taking some dreamsand from the flower petals that the old sandman had lavishly spread out before he noticed that the sand was running out. They were busily buzzing around and blown sand into the kids' eyes in order to help the sandmen, struggling to stay awake themselves. The old sandman smiled in relief. "See, everyone is trying to help us, it's wonderful!". The little sandman chuckled softly to himself, watching the dwarfs hurrying to fetch some water from the garden fountain and brushing the kids' teeth with strawberry toothpaste.

"Let's go now", the old sandman whispered, after thanking the dwarfs gratefully. "Next time we'll bring fresh dreamsand from the moon and you'll learn to act like a real, grown up sandman". After stepping back into their car, heading towards home, the old sandman reached into a tiny, emergency bag of sand and threw some grains over his shoulder. A moment later, he could hear his little son breathing softly, a smile still lingering on his dreamy little face.

Horse with a Flaming Eye (detail), oil on canvas

The Moon Pony

The little girl felt a bit sleepy after kindergarden so her Mum told her to rest for a while because she was planning to take her for a walk to visit the horses in the nearby meadow in the afternoon. The little girl was really excited because she loved the horses so much, she thought they were so beautiful. Their eyes always told her stories about a faraway land, a magical land which only a few special horses could find and which was kept secret by them - only very special friends were invited to share in the adventure with them.

The little girl gladly hopped into her wooden bed, deciding to look at her picture book again, the one she had been given last week for her fifth birthday, because she wanted to choose a pony for her afternoon dream ride. The book showed pictures of every type of pony, big ponies, small ponies, cute ponies, wild ponies, shaggy ponies, foals with toddling legs, ponies galloping over slight hills and ponies chasing each other on a sunny evening in front of a country farmhouse. There were black ponies and white ponies, yellow highland ponies, ponies with white stars on their noses, saddled ponies and foals taking a nap in their stables, cuddling up to their big parents placidly. There were ponies with orange carrots in their mouths, ponies with their heads stuck deep into huge water troughs and ponies grazing idly behind fences. There were ponies that looked quite weird because their forelocks covered their eyes and they had to stumble along blindly, wildly shaking their heads to and fro. Some ponies were playing in a group, others were standing apart silently gazing into the distance. And then there was a toy pony on a bed in one of the children's rooms in the country farmhouse in the book. It was a soft pony with intense eyes, its coat was so pitch-black it looked as if it was made of velvet charcoal. It had a bright red saddle on its back which looked as if it had been made for a wild little cowgirl. The girl rubbed her eyes drowsily and glanced longingly at the little black toy pony on page 12. Maybe Father Christmas would bring her a similar pony soon... It would be lovely to cuddle with the pony during her afternoon naps and have a friend to talk to at night before drifting off to the land of nod. The little girl got up, rummaged in a cardboard box and produced her crayons. With care and concentration, she held a black crayon tightly and started to sketch the pony she could picture in her imagination. It was, of course, only a toy pony but once it was on paper, like in the picture book, the little girl had noticed that everything came to life after a while ... as if the things and animals she had drawn were jumping out of the picture, or, even more weird, as if the girl herself was suddenly in the picture she had created. For a full hour, the little girl concentrated very hard, lying stretched out on the floor, the drawing pad before her. Her tongue appeared sometimes, moving quickly and nervously over her lips as if to judge the outcome of her efforts. The girl drew a soft little pony and coloured it pitch-black, like in her picture book. However, something was wrong with it, it seemed to be flying, not galloping. The girl thoughtfully viewed her sketch and decided it was a magical pony that could fly. "Why not?", she asked, happily smiling to herself. How lovely to paint a flying horse! But then, of course, it needed a pair of wings to carry it into the sky instead of stomping on solid ground. The girl looked at the pony for a while, and then added a pair of fine silver wings to its body. It looked funny and also very mysterious now. The girl chuckled and clapped her hands, thrilled and awed by her work of art. She continued by drawing a pale whitish-silvery moon, half hidden behind a grey cloud. The pony was given a ruby red saddle and soft brown eyes. "Will the pony fly to the moon?" the girl asked herself, curious. Suddenly, she felt as if the pony was talking to her, as if it had moved up higher in the painting to reach the upper end of the drawing pad. The girl rubbed her eyes in amazement and bent over the piece of paper to have a closer look. Indeed, the pony had spread its wings out and soared towards the silver moon that seemed to suddenly show its face from behind the big cloud. The girl rubbed her eyes again with her tiny little fist and pinched herself to make sure she was not dreaming. The cloud seemed to slowly change into the silhouette of a little cowgirl who was sitting in the pony's ruby saddle, her knees tightly pressed against the pony to stop herself falling into nothingness. The little cowgirl was wearing a real cowboy hat and cowboy boots and she smiled at the little girl who was standing looking at her speechlessly, holding her breath. Her eyes began to gleam in wonder because she somehow sensed that everything she drew was suddenly being transformed into reality. It seemed to be like a real dream, like moving toys in wonderland, or living dolls in the land of nod. Suddenly, a noise was coming from the open mouth of the little cowgirl on the page of her drawing pad. She seemed to have lost her balance when the pony was making a huge jump over one of the tinier white clouds in the picture. One leg had disappeared in the creamy silver mist and moon shadow so that the little cowgirl only seemed to have one leg. Of course she could not ride like that. She seemed to be frightened, her eyes questioning the little girl who, after all, was the artist and needed to decide what would happen now. The little girl scratched her head and started to talk out loud to the pony. She had secretly given the pony a name: Moon Pony, because it wanted to ride to the moon and was as mysterious as the moon itself. "Moon Pony", the little girl begged, "Could you trot a little slower and more evenly or something terrible will happen to the poor cowgirl. She is so shaken and afraid and has already lost one of her legs in the moon shadow! Only you can help her but you have to turn and ride back out of the dark side of the moon." The Moon Pony, however, didn't seem to be taking any notice of her or was simply ignoring the girl's plea. It began to jump even higher and more dangerously and suddenly tears were falling down the little cowgirl's cheeks in fear and terror. The little girl became desperate. She understood that the little cowgirl in the picture was strangely related to her own person and that the little cowgirl trusted her and was hoping that she would help to rescue her from this predicament. All of a sudden, the little girl had an idea. She took her rubber and started to change the Moon Pony's reins which the little cowgirl was holding tightly in her small fists. The girl shortened the reins and, reacting, the Moon Pony suddenly shied but slowed down, shaking its head wildly, coming to a halt only slowly. The girl smiled in relief. The little cowgirl gazed up at her with what seemed like a grateful expression in her big eyes, yet something was still wrong. The girl took a critical look and noticed that the cowgirl still had one leg missing, it must still be hidden in the shadow of the moon. "How can we remedy this?" the worried girl asked the cowgirl, scratching her head again. The cowgirl smiled reassuringly and pointed at the girl's rubber and pencil. "Oh, I understand," the little girl laughed happily, lowering herself onto the floor again in her favourite position to draw, taking the blue crayon now in order to draw another leg that was clad in blue jeans like the other leg, too. The little girl rubbed out parts of the moon shadow to make room for the second leg again, while the Moon Pony seemed to be standing motionless and mesmerized by the little cowgirl's firm grip, caught in the middle of moving forward, half touching the moon's surface. The girl took the opportunity to quickly finish the new leg and noticed that there was a bright smile on the cowgirl's face now, thanking her for her assistance. When the leg was completed, the girl leaned back with a satisfied nod. The cowgirl seemed to relax her grip on the reins a little bit so the Moon Pony could start to gallop again, high up into the sky of this wonderful land of adventure that the girl herself had invented on her drawing pad. She had a weird feeling as if a breeze had brushed her cheeks as the Moon Pony and the cowgirl passed her at full speed. She glanced at the page a second time and gave a short cry of disbelief. The Moon Pony and its rider had completely vanished... and all she could see now was the dark night sky she had drawn with some sparkling golden stars that were peering at her from laughing and curious faces. "Where are you?" the girl shouted... From afar, she could hear the distant neigh of the Moon Pony and the silvery timbre of the little cowgirl's laugh fading into another faraway world.

Dancing Shadows, oil canvas

The Star that Wanted to be Famous

nce upon a time there was a little star that shone brightly and proudly in the darkest of nights. He knew that he must be a very special star because his light radiated warmth and a nebulous softness, glowing like pure gold, and all the other stars that were the children of the Sun and the Moon envied him because of his very special garment. The little star shone over the driest of deserts but even so his luminous light was reflected a thousand times by a silvery lake there which served him as a mirror so he could contentedly look at himself sparkling and glimmering from above. Indeed, his starry attire was more beautiful than that of any other star child that lived in the vast galaxy and more glamorous than any princess' dress on Earth. While he was looking down at his own reflection in the lake, he started to dream about being the most famous star in the whole Universe. It would be wonderful to be famous and have millions of friends to play with, and the Sun and the Moon would be even more proud of his light that would shine like a firework of sparkling diamonds all over the night sky. The wind would blow over the lonely lake and create waves to demonstrate its awe and the little star would be able to move to the Seven Seas and gaze at his reflection in the Big Waters of the World instead of that quiet little desert lake. Millions of ships would sail under him and all of the sailors would look for his famous light that would save their lives on the darkest of nights because he would illuminate their way and guide them through dangerous rocks and reefs. They would name maps of the world after him and they would organize trips to the end of the world just to see him shining and shimmering. He would have friends from Russia, from America, and from Germany and all of them would visit him in their rockets and tell him how beautiful he was. The little star was still happily dreaming on when suddenly the wind really started to blow waves into the little desert lake and a ship came sailing along with a sailor on board who was gazing at the sky through a telescope. The little star became nervous, his beautiful glow flickered hesitantly and he tried to hide behind a big dark cloud but the wind blew harder and the skittish clouds moved away. The little star was paralysed with fear because of the sailor gazing upwards into the night sky. He was suddenly painfully unsure of his appearance and maturity, would his lustrous attire be fine enough to attract the traveller's attention? The self-conscious star felt very frightened and tried to dim his light and look for murkiness and shadows to hide behind for protection. The sailor below him fetched a map and scribbled something on it and kept gazing into the sky with great interest. In the meantime, the little star had noticed that he was the only star sparkling in the sky that night and he wondered why his brothers and sisters had not told him that they were not going to come out to shine as usual. "Is there something special about tonight?" the little star asked himself. "Have I missed some important news? Is this my night to be famous but alone? It's no fun being discovered if there's no-one else who wants to join me and become famous, too. I don't like this game any more and I miss my brothers and sisters. Why have they left me alone and what will the Sun and Moon say when they discover that I am not in my bed...?" At that very second and without warning the sky went pitch-black. The star started to shiver and cry in fear. His light was dim now and he felt like a little glowworm, lost in the big black Universe. "What has happened?" the little star wondered. He no longer wanted to be famous and he no longer wanted to move away from his family. He no longer wanted to gaze at his own reflection in the far and wide seas but just to dance in the night sky with his brothers and sisters and smile happily at his Mum and Dad whenever they came along. It was still terrifyingly dark and the little star continued to weep. "Have they all moved without telling me? I'm so scared and worried," he sobbed to himself. Down on the water, the sailor started to take a picture of the little star because his tiny light still visible. The area surrounding him was eerily silent and nothing could be seen except the pitch-black velvet dress of the night. Then the wind started to blow again and the clouds jostled their way back. They softly touched his golden attire that was now looking rather grey and worn out. "How beautiful you are," the clouds whispered. "How lovely and stunning you are if only you would stop looking down at the water and open your eyes wide and let them shine on us." The little star was confused and looked around him. "Are you talking about me? But I'm ugly," he contradicted. All of a sudden, he felt very ugly but at least not alone anymore, which was very comforting. "This is a very special night," the clouds whispered. "People call it an eclipse. It means your Mum and Dad, the Moon and the Sun, have found each other on their walk around the Universe and have fallen in love again and are now embracing each other lovingly. Your Aunt, the Earth, has made it possible for them to be alone for a little while because of her shadow , out of reach so no-one can disturb them for just a few moments in time. Isn't that beautiful and romantic... Now see how their soft red light is shining, they are making your attire shine red and golden like a million rubies … ." The little star was amazed and looked at the way his parents' love was reflecting on him to make him even lovelier than ever. He fell silent and simply listened to the night clouds' soft sighs. "How beautiful they are, too," he whispered, enchanted. And he was filled with pride to be a little unknown star, the child of such loving parents. "They will be famous," the clouds chuckled, "and you will be in the photo, too and then they will see that you hopped out of your bed tonight." The little star smiled, not the least bit worried. Now he would be famous with them, how beautiful and comforting it was to have such loving parents. He danced around happily the sparks that simply burst out of him touched the Milky Way where all the other little stars were dancing that night, with happy hearts, and no-one was envious because the little star told them how happy they should be to have such great parents whose love shone on and embraced all of them that people even came to the small desert lake to watch them kiss and how clever their Aunt had been to shield them from curious stares.

All paintings made by Jana Paul (oil on canvas)

Name of coverpainting: Swan lit by a Red Moon

www.poetic-oilart.de